Skydiving TO
Love

Linda W. Yezak

Skydiving to Love
Linda W. Yezak

Copyright © 2016
Linda W. Yezak

2nd Edition Copyright © 2018
Linda W. Yezak

Cover design by Indie Cover Design –
www.indiecoverdesign.com.

Skydiving to Love is a work of fiction. All characters, incidents, and dialogue are derived from the author's imagination. Resemblance to any event or person, living or dead, is purely coincidental.

Bible verses used in this work of fiction are taken from the New King James Version, Copyright © 1982 by Thomas Nelson.

Printed in the United States of America

Published by Canopy Books of Texas

ISBN-13: 978-0-9973336-5-7

Dedicated to all who take the faith leap into love.

"without faith, it is impossible to please Him."
Hebrews 11:6

Chapter One

*B*reathe. Just breathe.

JoJo Merritt squeezed her eyelids tighter and clamped her hands onto the armrests. *I can't.*

Inhale. There ya go. Good. Now exhale. Repeat.

What on earth had made her tell the girls that skydiving held top spot on her bucket list? As a veterinarian who owned a large animal practice, she was living her bucket list. Every calf she helped birth, every colicky horse she healed, fulfilled her dreams. But no—that wasn't good enough for her old college quartet. She had to do something totally off the charts. What on God's green earth had made her say skydiving?

The passenger jet's engines revved. Her breath jerked from her lungs. All around her, bored businesspeople and cool-as-a-Popsicle travelers settled in with magazines and headphones. But for her, even this simple, normal flight had been a disaster so far.

"You going to be okay?"

The deep voice next to her pierced her panic. She lifted one lid for a peek at its source in the aisle seat. Any other time—like when her stomach wasn't threatening to toss up everything she'd eaten in the past year—she would've found the man with the compassionate blue eyes attractive.

She slammed her lid shut. "I'm f-fine. Or I will be. Maybe. When we get where we're going and land and I'm still in one

Skydiving to Love

piece, I'll be fine. I-I think."

Great. She wasn't just stammering, she was throwing out more words than she'd spoken all week.

She peeked at him again. Great looking guy, square jaw, wavy dark hair. Too bad. If she didn't turn him off by tossing her breakfast, she'd do it by jabbering like an idiot.

His gentle laugh caressed her like a velvet glove. "You'll be fine. I know the pilot. Never lost a passenger."

Yet. He forgot the *yet*. Always a first time.

The plane began moving, taxiing this way, then that. She had no clue where because all she could see were the backs of her eyelids. Soon the engines pitched to a high whine and the plane moved faster and faster and she couldn't breathe and her heart lodged in her throat and threatened to choke her to death which didn't matter because she couldn't breathe. The engines roared, her brain screamed—

7

Skydiving to Love

Then the plane lifted, leaving her stomach back on the runway. No big loss. She was going to throw it up anyway.

They climbed and banked to the right. The engines fell quiet, and the muffled sounds of the other passengers reached through her fear. Her shoulders relaxed, her heartbeat returned to normal. Finally, she dared to open her eyes and look out the window. Puffy clouds drifted by, giving her only the occasional glimpse of the small towns and fields below. Before long, the ranchland scenery would shift to a cityscape as they flew over Austin and, soon after, over San Antonio. And then the pilot would land. God bless him.

"Feeling better?"

Mr. Dark-and-Handsome had traded the compassion in his eyes for humor. Kind humor, but humor just the same ... okay, no. He was laughing at her. Who wouldn't?

She flexed her cramped fingers and offered him a lame smile.

Skydiving to Love

"Yeah, I'm better. This is my first flight."

"It's not so bad once you get used to it." He poked his hand out. "Mitch O'Hara."

She shook with him. "JoJo Merritt."

"Where you from, JoJo?"

Small talk. They would now drift into small talk, something she'd blissfully avoided in her day-to-day life. She said she was from Hereford; he said he was originally from nearby Amarillo. She told him she was a large animal vet; he worked as a seismic engineer in San Antonio, where they were headed. She stifled a yawn.

Had she remembered her iPad, she could've tuned him out with a great audio book while watching the clouds below. But in her rush to get this week over with, she'd forgotten it.

At least he was nice to look at, animated as he described whatever project he spoke of. Intelligent eyes. Amarillo was near enough to Hereford, they could visit when he came home, yet far enough away not to stumble over each other. But it didn't matter. She wasn't looking for male companionship, just to finish her mission so she could head back to more earthbound things like cattle, horses, and goats.

"I've bored you enough with my business talk," Mitch said. "What about you? What are your plans while you're in San Antonio?"

His friendly chatter had kept her nerves calm during the bulk of the flight, but now, as they jetted over more densely populated areas, he decided to include her in the conversation. She sighed inwardly. Being rude was not an option.

"I've always wanted to see the River Walk," which was why she chose the jumping school there instead of the one in Dallas. "Maybe take in El Mercado."

"Sounds relaxing."

Skydiving to Love

Right. That part did sound relaxing. Jumping from somewhere in the sky, putting her trust in a parachute someone else packed—that *didn't* sound relaxing.

"Maybe I'll run into you," he said. "I know a great restaurant—Mi Tierra. Ever hear of it?"

She shook her head.

"You'd love it. They make the best pork dish I've ever eaten. Like pork?"

The fasten-seat-belt sign dinged and her stomach clutched.

"They have traditional stuff too. Enchiladas, tacos, nachos ..."

She felt queasy, was probably turning guacamole green.

"Great chicken dishes too."

The wings tilted to the left. The plane slowed noticeably. Taking off had been horrid. Being up hadn't been so bad—none of the plane-shuddering turbulence she'd heard of. But what would landing be like?

Skydiving to Love

"You do like Mexican food, don't you? I'm sure they have an American menu—"

"Please!" She shot her hand up and scrunched her eyes shut. "Just stop talking, okay? Please?"

"Oops. Sorry." Humor laced his voice again. Fine. Let him laugh.

The plane had tilted deeper to the left and slowed further.

She slipped her hands under her thighs to keep them from shaking and dared a glance out the window at the city below.

The city.

Highways. Neighborhoods. Schools. Businesses.

No runways. No place to land.

And the plane kept getting slower.

Was the pilot out of his mind? There was no place to land!

She hunched her shoulders forward. If she could close in on herself, turn herself into a tiny ball, maybe the impact wouldn't

Skydiving to Love

hurt so bad.

Well, that was stupid, wasn't it? The impact would kill her! They were all going to die!

Mitch chuckled and said something along the lines of everything being all right. At least that was what it sounded like. Hard to tell over the blood rushing in her ears and the relentless *we're-gonna-die* soundtrack.

The plane slowed more.

 Her hands fisted.

The plane leveled and dropped lower.

Her stomach leapt to her throat.

Where would they land? There'd been no airport, no runway in sight. Maybe if she opened her eyes, she'd see one.

No. No, this was fine. If they were going to crash, she'd just as soon not see the ground rushing up to greet her.

Dear Father in Heaven, open the gates, I'm coming home!

Skydiving to Love

The plane bounced slightly; the wheels screeched. The engine's whine dropped from a high-pitched squeal to a lower, though not soothing, tone. The passenger jet slowed more and more, until it felt like the speed of a Sunday drive. People rustled around her, anxious to get their gear from the overhead compartments and move on with their day's activities.

She just wanted the plane to stop so she could unclench her fists and catch her first glimpse of San Antonio. From the ground.

Mitch nudged her. "We're at the terminal."

With her stomach lodged in her throat, she could do nothing more to acknowledge him than nod crazily like a bobble-head.

"You can open your eyes now."

"Oh, okay." She'd had them squinched so tightly, the right lid began to twitch.

He stood in the aisle with his carry-on bag strapped over his shoulder. "Want me to get your bag?"

Skydiving to Love

"If you wouldn't mind." Maybe that would give her a moment to flex her cramping fingers.

The door opened, the flight attendant spoke unintelligible words through a scratchy intercom, and the restless travelers began to file out.

Mitch held up the line to let her in. "What did I tell you? We landed just fine. Flying's not so bad."

Matter of opinion.

She managed a feeble smile as she squeezed in front of him and followed everyone out and into the airport. Her nerves felt tight enough to tune, and her stomach threatened again. How would she survive skydiving if she could barely survive a simple one-hour flight?

Skydiving to Love

She rolled her suitcase far enough into her room to allow the door to close behind her, then dropped it and bee-lined toward the window. She'd spent a small fortune for a hotel right on the River Walk, though not enough of a fortune to get a river-front room. Still, when she drew the shades aside, she sucked in a breath. The city view was magnificent. And she could walk anywhere she wanted to go.

Except to the airport where she'd take her skydiving lessons.

She released the drape panel and dropped heavily into the cushioned armchair next to the window. The flight here had just about sapped every ounce of strength from her. Her fingers still felt gnarled from being clamped to the seat arms. How would she survive going up in a plane again, much less jumping out?

Her cell phone chimed, and she dug it out of her pocket.

A text from her college friend—and one of the ones who got her into this mess—Kat Brownlee. "U there & safe?"

Skydiving to Love

"Safe," JoJo typed.

"Ready for 2moro?"

"No."

"LOL. It'll b gr8. U'll see."

JoJo sighed. Having lost a limb while fighting in Afghanistan, Kat wouldn't likely understand her fear. Nothing scared Kat. Ordinarily, nothing scared JoJo either.

"GTG," she typed. "L8r."

She tossed her phone on the bed and stared at her suitcase. She might as well unpack. She'd be vacationing here for a week. Less, if the fall killed her.

Chapter Two

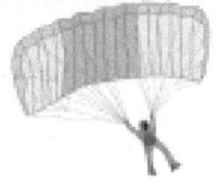

R efreshed from an afternoon nap and a long, back-pounding shower, JoJo sat at a table under a bright red umbrella at an outdoor café full of bright colored umbrellas. If she tuned out the buzz of the people around her, she could hear the river lapping against the restaurant's rock foundation.

Muscovy ducks swam as close as they dared and were rewarded with bits of bread tossed into the water. Terrible habit.

Skydiving to Love

Bread was bad for ducks. Made them heavy and fat, and didn't supply the nutrients they needed from their regular diet.

Still, they were cute to watch.

One timid hen held back from the rest of the squabbling quackers, nabbing only the occasional morsel tossed toward her. An aggressive drake charged her, his black, mottled neck and wings stretched as he squawked at her, but the splash from a chunk of bread nearby turned him from his attack. Soon, more bread landed closer to the hen, but away from the other ducks so she could have some of the treats to herself.

JoJo turned to see who threw the bread with such an expert arm.

Mitch grinned back at her. "Hey. I was hoping I'd run in to you again."

She scowled. "You shouldn't be feeding bread to the ducks. It's bad for them."

Skydiving to Love

"Yeah, but it's fun, and they seem to like it." He brushed crumbs off his hands, then grabbed his soda and strolled toward her. "Mind if I join you?"

Yes, she minded. She wanted the evening before her inevitable doom to be a calm, pleasant one. And as much as he talked, it would be anything but. All the ranchers and animals combined didn't talk as much as he did. But denying him a seat would be rude—especially since he'd already made himself at home.

"Good to see you survived the flight. Wasn't so bad, was it?"

She twirled a french fry in the dollop of ketchup on her paper plate. "Not bad, compared to having a tooth pulled without Novocain."

He clicked his tongue. "And to think you have to face another flight to get home."

"Oh, no. I rented a cute little two-door with great gas mileage and only forty thousand miles on it. I think I'll take it home with me." Eight hours behind the wheel, more or less, would get her home without seriously cutting into her vacation time, considering she'd spent almost that much time fighting airport traffic, checking her only suitcase, and going through security with her carry-on. Next time, she'd just drive her pickup.

Next time, she wouldn't take a vacation to jump from a plane.

Mitch gave a light snort. "I guess driving would be better on your nerves. If you can stand the traffic."

She nodded. "That may be an issue. In my normal life, I'm much more likely to be held up by a herd of meandering cows than slow traffic and crazy drivers."

"You didn't say much during the flight about your normal life. Actually, you didn't say much of anything." He leaned back in his chair and propped an ankle across the opposite knee as if he were settling in for a nice, long talk. "What's a normal day like for

Skydiving to Love

you?"

He appeared relaxed, interested. A casual conversation between friends. But she barely knew him, and chit-chat had always been impossible for her. Aside from her college buddies, her closest confidants had hooves and tails. Maybe he could open up and say moo.

"Oh, c'mon, now. Consider this payback." He grinned. "I must've bored you to tears with my stories when I was trying to keep your mind off the flight."

"Is that what you were doing?" How sweet! Not that it worked, but it was a nice gesture.

He shrugged a shoulder. "Since I travel a lot, I've come across a few people who are afraid of flying. Sometimes talking helps, sometimes listening helps. I do my part to keep them distracted."

"So you regale the poor, frightened folks with engineer talk and algebraic equations?"

Skydiving to Love

"Works every time."

Almost every time.

On the river, a crowded tourist gondola puttered past the restaurants and shops. Some aboard waved at those on more solid ground, others studied the shops and gazed at the ancient architecture. The gargoyles had captivated JoJo's attention also as she'd strolled along the river earlier.

Mitch nodded toward the tour boat. "It's not as romantic as the way the Venetians ride the waterways, but it still looks like fun. Want to try it?"

Eventually, but not as much as she wanted to just relax ... alone. Besides, with the sun setting and the lights from the surrounding shops beginning to reflect in the rippling water, the ride would seem too romantic to take with someone she'd just met.

"Hesitant?" His eyes held the glint of a challenge. "You're not afraid of water too, are you?"

"No, of course not. I was just thinking I'd turn in early. I had a busy day, and tomorrow will be just as busy." Not to mention terrifying.

"Oh, yeah. I understand that. I'm a little tired myself. What do you have planned for tomorrow?"

"Shopping in the Mexican Market, like I said earlier, and anywhere else that catches my attention." No way would she admit the truth of her plan to a man who knew precisely how ludicrous it would sound. "You know, girl stuff."

"The market is great. Maybe after my meeting, I'll find you there."

"Uh ... well, maybe."

He frowned and studied his soda cup. "Oh, I see. Not interested."

"Look. We just met. I don't even know you."

Skydiving to Love

"That's what we're doing here now, getting to know each other." He rose and pushed his chair to the table. "But I can take a hint."

With that, he strolled away. He tossed his paper cup into the nearest trash bin, then headed up a set of rock-slab stairs and out of sight.

Too bad. He was a nice guy. Good looking, too. Maybe she shouldn't have been so hasty. But she wasn't interested in a relationship. Didn't have time for one. Her days began before the sun came up and usually didn't end until well after dark. Overnight emergencies often interrupted sleep, which meant that her rare days off were usually spent dozing. She didn't have time for a man. Any man, much less one who lived so far away.

She pushed her own chair up to the table and headed in the opposite direction toward the hotel and the king-sized bed she'd rented for the week.

Skydiving to Love

Her cell phone rang out with "A Wink and a Smile," Annie Flowers' ringtone. Perfect timing. Another of the original college quartet, Annie made a living as a wedding photographer, so she had a soft heart for love and romance.

"How's the first day of your vacation going?" she asked.

"Well, I discovered flying terrifies me, found a great little outdoor café on the River Walk, and turned down a date with one of the best-looking guys I've seen in a long time. I guess you can say my vacation is just so-so."

"You get asked out your first day there, and your day's just so-so?" She tsked. "Girl, you need to re-assess your happiness scale."

JoJo turned on the sidewalk leading to her hotel and shook her head. "Maybe you didn't hear me. I am *terrified* of flying."

"Honey, if you can't fly in a plane, how are you going to jump from one? I thought this was on your bucket list."

Skydiving to Love

"That's just it—it *wasn't* on my bucket list." The entry doors to the hotel swooshed open for her, and she marched straight for the elevators. "I don't have a bucket list."

"You did back in college." Annie sighed. "So, what are you going to do?"

She punched her floor number, then flopped back against the wall and massaged her temples. "I'm going up. I mean, what choice do I have? If Kat is going to climb a mountain with her handicap, I'm going to skydive with mine."

"There you go. You can do this. And call me as soon as you do."

"Of course," if she lived through it. She signed off, headed to her room, and collapsed on the bed. With any luck, she wouldn't wake up.

Chapter Three

The orange windsock drooped from its pole at the small, community airport. That was a good sign, wasn't it? No wind to blow her into power lines, right? Or did that apply to hot air balloons?

Probably both.

She parked near the door sporting a US Parachute Association seal. Only a dozen or so other vehicles occupied spaces in the

Skydiving to Love

concrete lot outside the building, a far cry from the international airport she'd flown to the day before. The planes near the hangars were personal jets, gliders, bi-planes, and whatever other kind of small aircraft mankind had created. Nothing she wanted to jump out of. But if Kat could chase her dream, she could jump from a plane.

She had faced stubborn cows and high-tempered mules. She'd been stepped on, kicked, butted, bucked. She could do this.

She popped out of her rental and headed to the door before her pep talk could wear off.

Inside, a cute little brunette looked up from her fashion magazine. "Welcome to The Drop Zone. You signed up for classes?"

JoJo gave her name and presented her driver's license, then glanced around at the pictures hanging from the walls. Shots of bright canopies gliding through a clear blue sky, groups of jumpers holding hands to form a circle, goggled faces with expressions so excited, she could feel their ecstasy. Every picture presented people having a great time.

Of course. They wouldn't hang shots of bodies splatted on the concrete.

"Here you are," the receptionist said. "You're a little late, but not too bad. I just need you to fill out these forms before you join the class, and we'll be all set."

She handed JoJo a clipboard full of legal papers, including the promise not to hold the school or any of its instructors or pilots liable if the plane crashed or chute failed to open and she died on the tarmac—or something to that effect. Her hands shook as she signed the forms.

What on God's green earth had she been thinking? She could happily face her thirtieth birthday without having to jump from a plane, thank you very much. Couldn't they just throw themselves a party like normal people?

But a deal was a deal, and she'd given her word—something she never did lightly. If she said she'd do something, she'd do it.

Stupid bucket list.

Only one chair in the back of the orientation class remained unoccupied. JoJo slid into it. The eight attendees seemed to be in their late twenties, early thirties—around her age—but the instructor in the front hardly seemed old enough to shave.

He nodded at her. "Welcome. We were just getting ready to watch the video, so you didn't really miss anything."

The video lasted twenty minutes and included everything from putting on the harness to landing. According to the video, the first jump would be with an experienced partner. That was a relief.

Everything looked easy, so why were her palms sweaty?

When the video was over, the instructor rubbed his hands

Skydiving to Love

together. "Alrighty, then. Any questions?"

Yes. What was the mortality rate of this sport?

"No? Okay. Let's suit up and get ready for the tandem jump!" He pointed to a rack of yellow jumpsuits. "Don't forget your goggles. When you're dressed, come on out to the tarmac. We'll match you up with your partner and help you with your harnesses before we head over to the Twin Otter. Gonna be a great day for jumping, folks! See you outside."

JoJo leaned toward the young woman next to her. "Twin Otter?"

"That's the plane we'll be jumping from." She shoved her hand out. "I'm Heather."

"JoJo."

Heather had a friendly smile, obviously enhanced by a regular application of whitening strips. She'd pulled her chestnut hair into a ponytail, something JoJo should've done before she came. Too late now.

They walked together to the rack of jumpsuits. JoJo flipped through, looking for something that might fit her lanky frame decently.

"You ready for this?" she asked.

"Oh, yeah. I'm pumped!" Heather pulled out a suit perfect for her short stature and shoved a foot through one of the leg openings. "I've wanted to do this forever. First my parents wouldn't let me, then I couldn't afford it. But it's been a dream since I was a kid. What about you?"

"Not quite as enthusiastic." She picked a suit that looked to be her size. "I'm actually dreading it."

Heather gaped at her. "Seriously? Why would you come if you didn't want to?"

JoJo shrugged. "Kind of a dare."

"You're a brave one, then." Heather zipped up her suit. "I

can't imagine doing this unless I really wanted to."

She flipped her ponytail out from under her collar, grabbed some goggles, and offered a wave. "See you out there."

The others had dressed too and were heading out. Once again, JoJo would be late.

She rammed her feet through the jumpsuit legs and wiggled the suit up over her shoulders. The goggles had adjustable straps, so she grabbed the nearest and followed, zipping up her suit as she walked. She shouldered through the glass door and fumbled with the strap on goggles that had apparently been set to fit the Jolly Green Giant.

"I don't believe this."

Mitch's voice. She didn't even have to look up to recognize it, but she did—just in time to see him smirking at her.

Chapter Four

S he twisted her lips into what she hoped was a smile. "What are you doing here?"

He pointed his thumb over his shoulder, toward the instructor. "Chad needed an extra for the tandem jump. The real question is what are you doing here?"

"Yeah. Crazy, isn't it?"

"Downright insane." He brought her a harness. "You realize

37

you have to go in a plane, right?"

"I was hoping I could jump while it was grounded."

"Right. You paid two hundred dollars to jump seven feet?"

She sucked her lip between her teeth. Best not to answer and risk sounding more inane than she already did.

He shook his head and helped her with the harness, double-checking the straps to make sure they were secure. Then he gave her instructions about her harness and how it would connect to his. The concentration on his handsome face and the assurance with which he spoke and moved steadied her nerves.

When he was done, he propped his hands on her shoulders and searched her eyes. "You sure you want to do this?"

"Yeah, I guess," she answered, then lifted her chin and hooked her thumbs through the shoulder straps. She would do this, and she would do it well. She *could* do this. If he felt confident—and he would be the one holding on to her—then she

Skydiving to Love

felt confident. "Yes. I'm ready."

"Atta girl." He flashed a smile at her that warmed her insides. A smile of appreciation. Of admiration. For some silly reason, she wanted to live up to his new opinion of her.

But once they'd loaded into the plane and the engines flared to life and the twin propellers began to spin, her confident hold on the shoulder straps became a death grip. Though not as loud as the jet, the thrum of the propellers chopping the air vibrated down her back and stretched her nerves until they thrummed too.

Then the plane lifted, and her eyes slammed shut. An automatic response, apparently. She'd probably never go through a takeoff with wide-eyed eagerness.

More likely, she'd never go through another takeoff. Not if she could help it.

Mitch leaned against her shoulder. "It's going to be okay. This flight is much shorter."

Skydiving to Love

"Right. And it ends with me jumping out." She was crazy. Flat-out crazy. Out of her mind. Certifiably insane. "Is it too late to let me off?"

He shrugged. "Or too early. Take your pick."

"Ha. Ha."

He pried the fingers of her right hand off the strap and interlaced them with his own, rubbing his thumb soothingly over her knuckles. It helped.

"You really will love this," he said. "After a bit, when the wind noise is gone and it's quiet and peaceful, and you look at the beautiful patchwork quilt of this earth God created, you'll be happy you did this. Wouldn't surprise me if you wanted to do it again. Everyone does. But there's nothing like the first time. It's invigorating and awe-inspiring all at once."

The engine noise had either settled out, or she'd been concentrating on Mitch's gentle voice so hard, she'd drowned it out, but she was beginning to relax. The tightness in her shoulders loosened, her grasp on the harness strap began to ease. After a moment, she peeked at the other people on the plane.

The two groups faced each other on benches bolted down the length of the fuselage. Each novice sat beside an experienced jumper, and from what she could tell by their laughter and chatter, she was the only one with a knot in her stomach. Fortunately, they all seemed to concentrate on their own conversations, and no one cast condescending glances her way.

Soon, a yellow light flashed over the cockpit. Chad rose and went to the door in the side of the fuselage.

And opened it.

Was he crazy?

She clamped both hands on Mitch's arm. "What is he doing? We'll get sucked out of here! Won't we lose air pressure?" She scoured the ceiling with her eyes. "Where are the oxygen masks?

Skydiving to Love

Shouldn't they have fallen by now?"

"Relax. It's okay." He covered one of her hands with his. "We have to open the door. How do you think we're going to dive if we can't get out?"

"Oh." She released his arm and sat back. "Kind of silly of me, huh?"

His brow went up. "Kind of?"

The light above the cockpit changed to green, and Chad started shouting directions.

Heather and her partner were first in line. She shot JoJo a thumbs up and a broad, encouraging smile before moving closer to the gaping space in the side of the plane.

JoJo forced an upward lift to her lips in return, but didn't stand to join the others. Her legs wouldn't hold her up if she tried.

Mitch stood and extended a hand toward her. "You ready?"

"Um ... no. I'm good for now. I'll let a few of the others go

Skydiving to Love

first."

"Once Chad finishes the final inspection of all the harnesses, it'll go pretty fast. May as well get up and get inspected."

Chad had been walking down the line, jerking on harness straps, checking their security, and now walked to where she remained glued to the seat. He shouted over the wind noise, "You ready?"

No, she wasn't. She'd already answered that. But she stood and let the man with the baby face jerk on her straps. Then Mitch stood behind her and connected her to his harness, and Chad checked the straps again.

"Good to go!"

He returned to the head of the line and stood at the door, facing everyone. He held on to the frame and leaned out to look below, then he gave a series of signals—index finger up, thumb up, and a shouted *Go!*

Skydiving to Love

The first pair jumped, the line moved forward.

Chad lifted two fingers, then his thumb, then *Go!*

After a few seconds' hesitation, the second pair disappeared from view.

Funny. JoJo had expected screams of terror. Probably couldn't hear them over the sound of the wind whipping through the fuselage.

The third pair jumped. Four more before her turn.

She shifted her weight from foot to foot, then bounced on her toes.

Mitch held her down by the shoulders. "Be still. What you do, I have to do. We're connected, remember?"

Soon, the next to the last pair approached the door. The couple ahead of her moved forward, but her feet remained stubbornly riveted to the floor.

Mitch nudged her, prompting her to move, but she didn't

budge. Her body shuddered involuntarily, her teeth chattered until she clamped her jaw, but her feet refused to move.

"You okay?"

"No." She leaned back to talk into his ear. "I can't do this. I can't."

He rubbed her arms. "C'mon, give it a try. I bet you face things more frightening than this every day. Angry bulls, defensive sows. This is a cakewalk."

"Except I won't be walking, will I?" She'd be falling, from ten thousand feet. Only a third of what they'd been flying the day before, but still quite high enough to ensure a messy splatter when she belly-flopped to the ground.

The final couple moved ahead, leaving a long, empty space between JoJo and the gaping hole in the fuselage.

Chad waved them forward and shouted, "You're up."

JoJo shook her head and took a step back—or tried to. She

bumped into the solid rock wall of Mitch's chest, the unyielding form to which she was strapped.

Panic squirmed through her stomach and up her throat. The wind from the cavernous doorway couldn't cool the heat in her cheeks, heat that kept rising despite the distinct chill she suddenly felt all the way to her bones. Her hands sweated, her toes were like ice—and her head kept shaking no. No. *No!*

She twisted and jerked against the harness, against the straps holding her prisoner, and tried to free herself from Mitch.

He grasped her arms and slipped his leg backward to brace himself and keep them both from falling over. "Whoa, honey! Hold on—"

She fumbled with the clasps, her fingers so shaky she could barely control them. "No, no, no ... "

He reached around her and pinned her hands to her stomach, clutching her body to his. His arms felt like steel around her. She couldn't budge him if she tried, and she couldn't try because of his grip on her.

She whimpered and bit her lip against the tears threatening to fall. If she wasn't so terrified, she'd be furious—but one emotion at a time. First things first, and terror came first. She tried to scream, but nothing came out.

He squeezed her. "Can you hear me, baby? It's okay. Do you hear me? You don't have to jump. Okay? You don't have to jump."

"I-I don't?"

"No. You don't. We're going to land soon."

If he hadn't been holding her, she would've melted to the floor in a puddle of relief.

For the first time, she realized Chad was standing in front of her, his strong hands on her biceps, deep concern in his hazel eyes. How had she not seen him there?

Skydiving to Love

And another question—had it really taken two of them to hold her?

Chapter Five

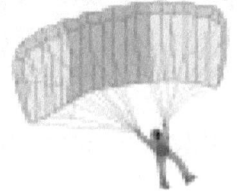

S he offered Chad a smile and a nod. "I'm okay now. I'm so sorry." She tried to twist around to extend her apology to Mitch. He relaxed his grip on her and stepped back.

They were no longer connected. That realization alone brought breath back to her lungs, but her legs felt wobbly and uncertain. She stumbled to the nearest bench and plopped down.

Chad sat beside her, and Mitch knelt in front of her, taking her hands. "That's one whopper of a phobia you have there, kiddo."

"Yeah, well, I didn't realize just how bad it was until I flew here. Back home, I'm never higher than horseback."

"We'll be landing soon," Chad said. "Glad you're all right. Don't sweat the jump. You're not the first who couldn't bring themselves to do it. It's a scary thing to a novice."

He patted her shoulder one more time, then headed for the cockpit.

"He's right," Mitch said. He lifted up and swiveled into the space on the bench Chad had vacated. "No shame in it. It's no big deal."

Then why did she feel like such a failure?

She'd given her word. Despite the fact she never should have spouted "skydiving" as top on her bucket list, she had given her word to the girls that she'd do it.

Skydiving to Love

And she failed. She couldn't even say she'd tried. She'd just stood at the back of the plane in a quivering panic. How could she tell them? She couldn't try again some other time—her bank account was too low for her to frivolously slap down another two hundred dollars.

The plane landed, but she couldn't convince herself to get up. How could she face Heather and the others? What kind of looks would a coward get—sneers or pity? Would they regard her at all?

They were probably having too much fun reciting the details of their jumps to each other to notice her. Maybe she could slink into the classroom, return the jumpsuit, and slip out without notice.

"Let's just sit here awhile." Mitch closed his eyes and leaned back. "Let me catch my breath. Nothing wears a man out faster than battling a hysterical woman." He peeked at her with one eye.

Skydiving to Love

"Even if she's pretty."

"I don't know whether to thank you or smack you." Though *hysterical* described her perfectly. She leaned back too, her shoulder rubbing against his. "Thank you."

Before long, Chad poked his head into the cabin. "Figured I'd find y'all in here. C'mon. I need to close up shop. Everyone's gone but you two."

Mitch gave her a hand up. "I'll help you get out of your gear if you'll drive me back to town."

"How'd you get here?"

"With Chad. But I'd rather leave with you."

She shot out a breath and tried to smile. "I guess that's the least I can do, since you've been so nice and all."

"Heroic. That's the word you're looking for." He grinned, broad and toothy. "Admit it. I'm your hero."

She gave an exaggerated roll of her eyes. "Yeah, yeah, you're my hero. Let's get out of here."

As they headed back into San Antonio, JoJo began to relax—at least from her failed attempt at jumping. The crazy traffic brought its own tension. But the GPS gave her a sense of confidence and being on the ground gave her a sense of relief.

Mitch had sprawled comfortably in his seat, one arm along the side window and the other stretched to the back of her headrest. With eyes the color of the sky they'd just flown in, the man was definitely handsome. But more important, he seemed to have a compassion about him she appreciated. No doubt in her mind he hadn't needed that rest from wrestling with her near as much as she'd needed it from being hysterical. In fact, everything he'd done since she met him smacked of understanding and empathy. The man seemed downright perfect, though he was bound to have some flaws. Everyone did. But still, he'd be a great catch if he didn't live so far away—and if she was actually looking for a great catch. Who had the time?

She made a turn, and traffic intensified.

"Where we headed?" Mitch asked.

"El Mercado. I'm taking you up on your offer last night to join me." She flashed him a smile. "I assume your meeting is over?"

"Yeah, and it left me famished. Let's eat first."

They agreed on Mi Tierra, a loud, bustling restaurant decked out with colored, twinkling lights and vibrant decorations. Every inch a tourist trap, but the food was remarkable, even if the noisy atmosphere didn't allow for intimate conversation. They stopped by the bakery for dessert, then headed toward the market. JoJo unwrapped the tissue from her *cocada* and bit into the sweet coconut candy as they walked.

Mitch elbowed her lightly and pointed to a pottery display.

Skydiving to Love

"Looks like something you'd like."

A ceramic colt sat on the shelf—dark blue head, olive green ears, rust-colored mane, red legs, and vivid blue flowers on his sides. Traditional Mexican art, beautifully crafted. And it stole her heart away.

"Oh, you're right. I love it."

But one look at the price tag had her backing away from the store.

"Sorry," Mitch said. "I didn't realize it would be so high."

The price wasn't *that* high, really, just more than she could afford, what with the room she'd splurged on and the jumping lessons she'd blown good, hard-earned money on. Between the rent on her farmhouse and her college loans, she couldn't afford impulse buying.

The next store featured sombreros and serapes. Mitch grabbed a bright red sombrero with an ornate golden design and plopped it on.

He lifted both arms to the right side of his head, snapped his fingers, and shouted, "*¡Olé!*"

"That looks great on you." Actually, it made his head look small and hid his handsome features in shadows. She couldn't help giggling.

He danced to the background music, a clumsy salsa to the Latin beat pulsating through the store. She found a dark green sombrero sporting a design in gold and white, then mimicked his movements, throwing in a few of her own.

How crazy to be dancing in the middle of the store like this, but she couldn't help it and refused to be embarrassed. She hadn't felt this carefree in ages.

He found a serape with colors that matched both her green sombrero and his red one, and draped it around her shoulders. "Perfect."

Skydiving to Love

He held her in his gaze, his laughter reflected in his eyes. Then something else shadowed those beautiful blues. Something she recognized. She caught her breath as he gently lifted the hat from her head. Her focus shifted to his lips as they came closer to her own. Her senses buzzed, her heart raced—how long had it been since she'd been kissed?

But she'd known Mitch all of two days.

She laid a hand on his chest. "People are staring."

"Let them," he whispered, coming closer still.

She turned her head. "Mitch ... Not yet. Not now."

He kissed her temple, caressed her cheek. "I won't apologize for wanting to."

"You don't have to." She slipped the serape from her shoulders. "I'd better put this up."

He put the sombreros away. "I'm thirsty. You thirsty?"

"Parched." Her mouth had dried the moment she realized he

intended to kiss her. "I could go for a lemonade."

They wandered the plaza until they found a quaint snack bar housed in a turquoise-colored stucco building. She ordered her lemonade, and he ordered a soda and a side of nachos. They took their treats to a table near the window.

"I've been curious about something." She used her straw to stir her drink and glanced at him from under her lashes. "You seem to understand the fear of flying."

"Well, I should. I was worse than you are."

"Really? How did you get over it?"

He pulled a nacho chip from the cheese and plopped an extra jalapeño on it. "I joined the Air Force."

She choked on a sip and covered her mouth to cough. "You're joking. That seems a bit counterintuitive, doesn't it?"

"It worked. Faced my fear head on in an environment where you don't admit you have any fears. Started out right here, at

Skydiving to Love

Lackland Air Force Base. Loved San Antonio, which is why I came back to live."

"Did you have to fly often?"

"Chose to." He wiped his fingers on a napkin. "Once I got over the fear, I became a pilot. Nothing glamorous, just an airbus. I hauled people and cargo wherever they told me to go, then I got out. Finished college, got my engineering degree—and there ya go. My life's history."

"Sounds interesting."

"Sounds very much like the same thing I told you on the plane. It's your turn now. Tell me about yourself."

She shrugged. "Not much to tell. I live in a rented farmhouse outside of Hereford, and I tend sick animals for a living. That's pretty much it."

"Why'd you become a vet?"

"I've always loved animals. They're fun and funny and often

far more deserving of my care and attention than people."

"Ouch." He popped another nacho in his mouth. "That's not a very optimistic view of the human race."

"Well, what can I say?" She sipped her lemonade.

"So why did the vet decide to jump from a plane?"

She released a sigh. "It was silly, really. My friends and I are all turning thirty this year, and they wanted to do something truly daring. Years ago, we'd made up bucket lists—or they did. I never took it seriously. Our birthday dare is to actually do the biggest thing on the list. Annie is going to crash a Hollywood wedding, Arabel is heading to Scotland, and Kat ... well, Kat lost her leg in Afghanistan, which killed her dream of being a mountain climber. But she decided she would try it anyway."

"What about you?"

"I couldn't think of anything when they pressed me on it this past spring, so I blurted the first thing to pop in my head."

Skydiving to Love

"Skydiving."

She sighed again and nodded. "Skydiving. Is that not insane?"

"It is if you're afraid to fly."

"I didn't know I'd respond that way yesterday until they closed the hatch."

His brows drew together, and he leaned forward with his forearms on the table. "What if I could get you over your fear of flying?"

"I'm not sure that's possible. You saw me up there. I was a lunatic."

"Not a lunatic, just scared. How long will you be in San Antonio?"

"After what happened today, I should go home tomorrow, but the room is booked until Friday."

"That's plenty of time. I'll pick you up in the morning. Where are you staying?"

Skydiving to Love

She gave the hotel name, then tilted her head. "What are you going to do?"

He rubbed his hands together and effected the look of a silent-movie villain. "You'll see."

"I don't like surprises," or anything else she couldn't control.

"You'll like this one."

Chapter Six

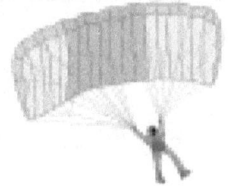

He had given her no clue what they'd be doing today, so if her red tunic belted over skinny jeans didn't appeal to him as he scoped her from head to foot, it was his own fault. She crossed the hotel lobby and stood in front of him.

"Well? Do I meet your approval?"

"Sensible shoes." His eyes held a glint of appreciation, defying his pragmatic tone. "That's good. And no purse. That's good too."

She flicked her belt over at her waist to show the zippered pocket on the underside. "Just the necessities."

"Girl after my heart." He waved toward the entrance. "Ready?"

She walked ahead of him and through the doors. A denim-blue Audi TT-RS, polished to a high gleam, sat in the circle drive. She'd seen it only in commercials. It had class, sass, and one powerful engine. Back in college, when she wasn't daydreaming about a four-door, full-bed pickup, she'd dreamed about this baby.

And Mitch just opened the passenger door for her. What a man.

She climbed in and smoothed her hand against the tan leather. No ranch grit here. No smell of hay and manure. No blood or medicine stains. Pure luxury.

Skydiving to Love

He settled behind the wheel and waved toward a couple of tall, paper cups in the holders. "Did you have your coffee this morning?"

"Yes, but I'm always game for another." She opened the drink spout and sniffed. "What is it?"

"It's a blonde roast. A little milk, a little sugar, some hazelnut." He shrugged. "I figured if you hadn't already tried it, you may like it."

She tasted and licked her lip. "I do."

"Good." He fired up the engine. "Top up or down?"

"Down. Great car."

"Yeah, she's a little old, but I can't part with her."

He merged into traffic, and soon jetted down the on-ramp to I-37 and slid with ease onto southbound lane.

"Where are we going?"

He leaned toward her. "What?"

Skydiving to Love

She raised her voice over the wind. "Where are we going?"

"Oh." He shifted lanes and sped up. "I thought we'd go on a tour of the Catholic churches in town. Do you like history?"

"Yeah, but what about getting me over my phobia?"

"We'll get to it."

They'd hit the highway late enough in the morning that whoever needed to get to work had long ago arrived at their destinations. Other than a few eighteen wheelers, service vehicles, and the odd passenger car, the interstate seemed fairly clear. Mitch darted around a poky U-Haul and cranked up the speed.

"We in a hurry?"

"Nope."

She peeked at the speedometer. Eighty and climbing. Excitement bubbled up from her toes and released on a giggle. "Let her roll!"

Skydiving to Love

She'd always wanted to see what this baby could do. The road ahead was clear for quite a way, and the wind through her hair felt great. She tilted her face toward the sun and reveled in the car's speed and power. She rarely cranked her old work truck over sixty—couldn't afford the wear and tear that the state's speed limit of seventy-five threatened. But riding in the Audi was every bit as good as racing full-gallop across an open pasture.

Far too soon, they slowed for the exit, and the thrill tapered off. By the time they entered city traffic, she felt they were crawling along at ten miles per hour. Forty felt syrupy slow.

Finally, they turned to the manicured grounds of an ancient, stone mission. Old buildings held new purposes—a visitor's center, a public restroom. But the mission and its trio of bells stood majestically silhouetted against a cobalt sky.

"It's beautiful."

"San Juan Capistrano, the Texas version. Spanish Franciscans built it around 1731. Back in 2000, a bunch of idiots stole some artifacts from the sanctuary. Priceless statues carved from wood back in the Spanish Colonial period. They ought to be horse-whipped."

They followed the modern sidewalk through antiquity, stopping for a moment at Tierra Sagrada, "Sacred Earth," an unfinished church from 1780.

"This is where a lot of the folks from that day are buried," Mitch said. "Want to go into the old mission?"

"Of course."

The temperature dropped considerably inside the stone structure, and the silence seemed almost holy. Their footfalls on the worn brick floors made virtually no sound, but even the gentle pad of their steps felt sacrilegious, intrusive. Wooden pews sat in two rows on either side, and hewn beams held up the ceiling. The statuary near the altar was beautiful in its simplicity. What a contrast to the outside world.

After a few moments, he gestured her back outside. "You've got to see this."

Standing as close as possible to the building, he pointed up to the iconic bell tower, with its three bells, each hanging under its own stone arch. She tilted her head far back and studied them from this angle—what she could see of them.

"Wouldn't it be easier to see them from over there?" She glanced around and found him studying her as if she were some laboratory specimen. "Something wrong?"

He shook his head. "Ready to go?"

She shrugged off the feeling that he was examining her and followed him.

They didn't drive far to their next stop, the walled Mission San Jose, an incredible specimen of 18th Century Spanish architecture, although repaired and renovated over the years. The arched walkways, the domed roof over the cathedral, the rose window. Sculptures of the saints adorned the front of the mission.

So ornate. So beautiful.

Mitch nudged her. "Want to go up in the bell tower?"

Of course she did. "Can we?"

He put a finger to his lips, then whispered, "C'mon."

They climbed the age-worn, wooden stairs to the belfry and made their way to a spectacular view of the grounds with its surrounding stone buildings and gnarled trees.

Mitch stepped close to one of the arched openings and pointed at the low structures bordering the mission complex. "Those used to house the Native Americans who lived and worked on the mission. It's amazing how many came to Christ during the era all these churches were—Oops."

She faced him. "What's wrong?"

He pointed toward the ground directly beneath them. "See

Skydiving to Love

that?"

She glanced down. "What?"

"I dropped a quarter. Do you see it?"

Laughing, she leaned over farther and searched the grass and shrubs below. "Don't see it. I hope that doesn't break you. It's a goner."

"I needed it to help pay for lunch." He grinned and a spark of mischief brightened his gorgeous blue eyes.

A good-looking history buff-slash-engineer-slash-skydiver with a great personality. And he was spending the day with her. Maybe Annie was right. She needed to readjust her happiness scale.

He led her down to the ground floor and outside the mission. "I have one more place to take you, then I have meetings for the rest of the afternoon. But let's eat first. You about ready for lunch?"

Skydiving to Love

"Sure. Where are we going?"

"I'm hungry for a burger. What about you?"

"You know what I mean." She shoulder-nudged him as they walked to the car.

He laughed and pretended to trip sideways.

"A burger's fine," she said, "but where are we going after?"

"You'll see."

After several minutes of darting through traffic and sitting at red lights, she finally realized where they were headed. At least, she hoped they were going there—the Tower of the Americas. The Texas version of the Space Needle. It had been on her list of things to see while in the city, and now, not only would she get to see it, she would be with someone whose company she had learned to enjoy.

She glanced at him from the corner of her eye. He chatted away about the area's history and the missions they'd missed seeing, but the wind blew most of his words away. He looked casual in pressed khakis and a button-down shirt with the sleeves rolled up to his elbows. Aviator glasses kept the sun from his eyes, and the wind sifted through hair that probably would have curled if allowed to grow longer. He kept his left hand on the wheel and the right resting on his thigh. What would happen if she picked that hand up and traced the veins ...

What a ridiculous thought. She'd just met him.

He found the nearest parking spot and nodded toward the tower. "What do you think? Are you game?"

"Absolutely!" She climbed from the car before he had a chance to cut the engine.

"Hang on," he called. "I'm coming."

They crossed under the arched Tower of Americas sign and over the paving bricks toward a cute little glassed-in café with outdoor seating—perfect for a day like today.

Skydiving to Love

"Is this where we're having lunch?"

"Nope. I thought we'd eat at the Chart House."

"Oh. Okay." She bit back her disappointment. "Is it near here?"

That mischievous glint lit his eyes again, and he pointed skyward. "About seven hundred fifty feet straight up."

Disappointment steamed away when her excitement boiled over. "I'd heard about the observation deck and the view from the elevator while going up, but whoever told me about those neglected to mention a restaurant up there."

"They have a burger that'll make your tongue sing." He rested his hand on her back and guided her through the crowd. Apparently he already had tickets—how long had he planned this? "Do you like blue cheese?"

She nodded as they worked their way into an elevator.

"Then you'll love this hamburger—grilled to perfection and

served with this incredible bacon marmalade. Do you like bacon?"

"Who doesn't? Never heard of it as a marmalade before."

The elevator lifted and soon the downtown area came into view. Modern buildings overshadowed the old and historic, new construction promised a future. In the distance, vehicles zipped down the highway. If the Franciscan monks could've seen this place now.

They strolled the tower's glass observation deck for a panoramic view of San Antonio. Occasionally, Mitch would rest his hand on her shoulder or back and point to something. The warmth of his touch distracted her to the extent she couldn't concentrate on what he said. Good thing he didn't intend to quiz her.

Sitting across the table from him now, she felt a strange sense of loss. He sat all the way over there. If she reached out far enough, she could touch him, but casual contact across a two-foot expanse didn't seem as natural as when they'd been standing side by side in the observatory. Still, there was always the tight elevator ride back down.

They finished their burgers—or she ate as much as she could and requested a doggie bag for the rest. He hadn't been kidding about it being the best in the city. Bacon marmalade. Who knew?

"I have to take you back to the hotel and go to my meeting this afternoon." He took a sip of his tea and leaned back in his chair. "But I'm happy to say that you've just about completed the test. You're zipping through it with flying colors. Pun intended."

"What test?"

"I'll fill you in later, provided you'll have dinner with me."

She reached for her glass. "You're going to make me wait after you've piqued my interest? That's just cruel."

"Well, the test isn't over yet."

Skydiving to Love

"Okay. What's left to do?"

"You'll see. If you have dinner with me."

She'd see? She hadn't seen anything yet that indicated she'd been tested. Not knowing what would happen from one moment to the next grated against her control-freak nature, but she'd enjoyed his company—and his casual caresses—all morning. Who knew what the evening would hold?

She squinted at him. "And you'll explain what you're talking about?"

"Absolutely."

"What time?"

"Sun sets at nine. Can you wait that long?"

She held up her carry-out box. "If not, I have something to tide me over."

Chapter Seven

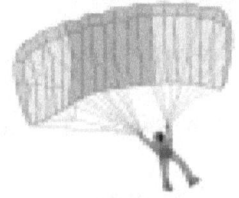

The only hint Mitch had given JoJo before dropping her off at the hotel left her no clue where they'd be having dinner: "It may be a little cool." Texas summers were never cool—even night temps hovered around the mid- to upper-seventies—so perhaps the restaurant had a strong air conditioner. But which restaurant?

Skydiving to Love

She'd spent the afternoon shopping the sales for a dress that could be considered casual enough for a burger joint and dressy enough for someplace high-class and fancy, and something to drape around her shoulders if she really did get cold. She'd found a slinky turquoise shift with spaghetti straps and a crocheted salmon-colored shawl. Something totally different from her usual style of jeans, boots, and tees with the sleeves rolled up. As long as she remembered not to walk like a bow-legged rancher dodging cow patties, she'd do great.

Shoes would make the difference for the evening—slip on ballet flats, and she'd look casual; with heels, she'd look ready for the society pages. She'd bought a pair of each. Now if she only knew which to wear.

She checked her hair and makeup in the mirror again, then checked the clock. He'd be in the lobby any moment. The dress looked great, the inexpensive bangle earrings she'd bought tickled her neck. Her makeup looked pretty good for someone who almost never wore it. Wherever he planned to take her, she would certainly wow him. And for the first time in her adult life, she really wanted to wow a man—this man.

If she only knew which shoes to wear.

She hated not being in control. If she'd been in control—or at least had enough information to make an intelligent decision—she'd know which pair to put on.

The room phone rang, and she hurried from the bathroom to grab the receiver.

Mitch's baritone voice greeted her. "You ready?"

She glanced at her new shoes sitting beside the bed. Decision time ...

"Yes."

She rode the elevator down to the lobby, then crossed toward him on the polished floor in her bare feet. She held the flats in one hand and the sling-back pumps in the other. "Which do I wear?"

He appraised her with a luscious gleam in his eye. "I like you just as you are."

"Uh-uh, buddy. I'm not going anywhere barefoot." She raised her hands. "Pick."

He laughed and pointed to the flats. "Those would probably be best."

"Good." She balanced herself on his shoulder as she slipped them on. "I was dreading the heels anyway. Haven't worn them in years. Not much call for fancy shoes in the pasture."

She left the other pair with the lady at the desk, then took Mitch's proffered arm. "Where are we going?"

"You'll see."

"That's maddening. You know that, right?"

"Don't like surprises?"

Skydiving to Love

The doors swished open, revealing the Audi. Hot car, hot man—hot ideas of kisses and caresses that had rarely entered her mind. She was in unfamiliar territory. But she liked it.

As he helped her into her seat, she gave him her best smile and hoped it wasn't too rusty. "I'm learning to love surprises."

He drove a few blocks and parked near a high-rise surrounded by other high-rises, all of which looked like they housed offices. "Here we go."

"There's a restaurant around here somewhere?"

"So to speak."

They left the car, entered the building, and strolled to the bank of elevators in the back of a marble-floored lobby lined with closed doors and darkened, etched windows. If there was a restaurant in this building, it must've had an amazing ventilation system. She smelled nothing more than the antiquity found in most old buildings.

Skydiving to Love

She slanted a look at Mitch, but didn't bother asking again where they were going. The man wanted to surprise her. She'd let herself be surprised.

The elevator stopped at the top floor, but he punched a key and entered a number on the pad, and the car lifted again—not far, maybe just one more floor. The doors opened into darkness. Only a red security light brightened a metal utility door.

He waved toward the door. "We're here."

She didn't budge. "We're where, exactly?"

He rested his hand on her lower back and urged her forward. "Not going to find out standing in the elevator."

The metal door opened to the rooftop and a stunning lavender and rose sunset.

Mitch guided her left, past the little building housing the elevator access and to a small table set for two, its white cloth lifting lightly in the breeze. Oil lanterns hung on ornate wrought-iron stands, casting a gentle golden glow over the setting. On one of the china plates, two roses rested, one yellow and the other red.

He picked them up and handed them to her, yellow first, "for friendship," then the red, "for romance."

Words escaped her. She buried her nose in the petals, then peeked up at him. "This certainly is romantic."

The table had been set close to the roof edge, providing them a clear view of the river and the city lights. He pulled her chair out for her, and white-jacketed waiters she hadn't noticed came to pour water and serve salads.

She thanked them, then draped her napkin over her lap and glanced at Mitch. "You certainly know how to pull off a surprise."

"I had fun planning it, I have to admit." His lips quirked up at the corners. "Even if it is part of the test."

Skydiving to Love

"Ah. The test. You going to finally tell me what that's all about?"

He leaned forward. "I wanted to pinpoint just what it is about flying that scares you. Can't be the speed. Judging from the way you reacted to our drive this morning, you're a speed demon yourself. You don't seem to have vertigo. You looked straight up at those bells of St. Juan Capistrano and didn't once seem dizzy."

"No, I've never had vertigo."

"And though the idea of the jump rattled you, you don't seem to be afraid of heights. The Tower of the Americas didn't faze you. But the observatory is enclosed in glass. Here, there's nothing between us and the concrete sidewalks but a short, brick barrier. You seem fine with it."

"Wait a minute. You mean all this"—she waved her hand over the formally set table—"is just part of a test?"

"Yes ... and no." He took her hand. "I made myself clear the other night that I wanted to get to know you better."

He traced circles in her palm, causing her heart to race. How was she supposed to think with him making her light-headed and muddle-brained?

She slipped her hand away and lifted her water goblet. So the day was part test, part date. She could live with that. "Okay, so let's talk about the test. Speed doesn't bother me, I don't have vertigo, and I'm not as afraid of heights as I'd thought. So where does that leave us?"

"You have to tell me." He sat back. "What was going through your head when we flew down here? What bothered you most?"

"Everything. All of it. The noise especially. That horrid engine whine on the jet."

"The whine ... " He drummed his fingers on the table. "You're from Hereford, right?"

She nodded.

Skydiving to Love

"You're a vet? You work on ranches and such, right?"

"Yes, and I see what you're getting at. I live a pretty quiet life. Tractors and old trucks don't get quite as loud as jet engines."

"So it makes sense that the noise would get to you. And, I guess if you're already anxious about the noise, the idea of the jump just compounded the problem."

She shook her head. "I think it's the other way around. I came here with the notion that jumping is insane. I'd been dreading it since I first agreed to do it. I didn't know about flying or the engine noise until I was strapped to the seat."

"Let's take first things first. We need to get you over your fear of flying." He continued to drum his fingers on the table, studying her with an untrustworthy gleam in his eye. Then he shifted his gaze to the space just over her left shoulder.

She squinted at him. "What are you thinking?"

"That you'd like flying if it wasn't for the noise."

"Well, that's moot. Engine noise comes with the territory, doesn't it?"

"Not always. Not so bad." He grinned. "Not in a Piper Cub."

Chapter Eight

S tanding outside a metal hangar the next morning, JoJo shielded her eyes against the sun and stared at a clunky-looking, single-wing prop plane with a green stripe down its side. Mitch must've been kidding. This two-seater seemed barely larger than one of those remote-controlled things kids played with.

He patted the fuselage. "What do you think?"

Skydiving to Love

"Does that thing fly?"

"Of course it does."

She shook her head. "If I freaked out in the Twin Otter, what makes you think I won't freak out in this?"

"You're not jumping out of this."

He had a point.

He crooked his finger, beckoning her closer. "C'mon. Let me introduce you."

As small planes went, it was a pretty thing for all its girth. Not streamlined like the Twin Otter, but it was clean.

She walked around to the right side and pointed at the name painted on the door. "Mary Beth?"

"My mom. She died before I got out of the Air Force."

"Sorry," she said. "Nice tribute."

"Thanks." He held open a half-door and offered his hand. "Ready?"

Skydiving to Love

"I guess so."

He showed her how to climb in. "You're in front."

"How will you be able to see?"

He chuckled. "Don't worry. I'll be fine."

She settled on the stitched leather seat with one leg on either side of a joy stick just like the one at the back seat. The control panel in front of her held a compass, an analog clock, and gauges for fuel, altimeter, and things unfamiliar to her. After Mitch helped her strap in, she tucked her feet close and slipped her hands under her thighs so she couldn't accidentally touch anything.

He climbed to the back seat, then unlatched the plexiglass side-window from its hook on the wing and let it drop, closing them in. The propeller flipped to life, cutting the air with distinguishable chops until it picked up speed and sounded as blurred as it looked.

Skydiving to Love

He tapped her shoulder, handed her a set of headphones, and yelled, "Put these on."

She settled them over her ears, and the prop and engine noises disappeared.

"Better, isn't it?" His voice came through the headset as clearly as if they were sitting side by side in a quiet theater. "Pull the mike down and we can talk."

She lowered it toward her lips and spoke in a normal voice. "This is great."

"Yeah, beats shouting at each other." The plane started moving down the tarmac toward a turn-off, heading who knew where in this maze of concrete. "Bear with me while I talk to the tower."

All the jargon between Mitch and the air-traffic controller floated through her headset. She understood little of it until they finally reached a long runway, and the controller said, "Clear for

Skydiving to Love

takeoff."

She balled her fists and squeezed her eyes shut, waiting for the noise to penetrate her nervous system. The plane rumbled down the runway, gaining speed, but was up far sooner than she expected. She peeked out the windshield. There was still plenty of runway left, but they were already climbing into a clear blue sky. The tower disappeared over her shoulder as they banked and headed northeast.

Was the flight really this quiet?

She freed her right ear from the headset. The usual wind noise, the gentle chugging and hum of the engine—all at a speed slower than their drive down the freeway in his Audi. If she wasn't careful, she'd learn to enjoy this.

The plane soon leveled, though nowhere near the altitude they'd been at in the Twin Otter. "How high are we flying?"

"Current cruising altitude is two thousand feet, at a nice

leisurely pace of sixty-five miles per hour. Perfect for a tour around the city. How's it going up there? You good?"

"Yes. I'm good." And she was. As relaxed as she would've been on horseback. "This is really nice."

"We can fly farther out, if you'd like."

"I think I'd like that. I've seen all the buildings I care to."

He took the plane to a higher elevation. The propeller spun, the engine chugged, and the plane leveled again.

After a while, he said, "We're flying over New Braunfels now. Pretty town. Those rivers running through it are the Comal and Guadalupe. Keep following Interstate 35 down there, and we'll end up in Austin. Of course, before we get there, we'll pass a great outlet mall that covers several acres. Want to see it from the air?"

Even more parking lots and buildings? She'd seen enough of both as they flew out of San Antonio. "No, that's okay."

Skydiving to Love

He shifted the plane west, leaving the interstate behind. Before long, he said, "See that water tower? That's the famous tower of Gruene, Texas. I don't think there's more than a hundred people who live there, but the population swells during tourist season because of its shops and wine tastings."

"That's nice."

He chuckled. "Not too impressed, are you?"

"Well, it's okay. I've just never been one to shop." She'd met her quota when she bought her dress for last night.

"Are you nervous up here? Scared?"

"No, I'm enjoying myself. I think you were right about the noise."

The sun glinted off the blue waters of a lake in the distance, and she pointed toward it. "What's that?"

"Canyon Lake. My folks bought a condo there when I was in the Air Force. We still have it—right on the water. Dad comes and stays there now and then. Supposed to come down this weekend."

Shaped roughly like a salamander, it looked like it had several coves just perfect for bass fishing. Seeing them from the air as they neared, she could almost pick which would be the hottest spot. "Can we get closer to the water?"

The wings tilted and the Piper Cub lowered into a slow curve down toward the lake.

He pointed to a set of docks with walkways leading up to a series of buildings. "Our place is in there."

"Why don't you live out here?"

"Can't get my pizza delivered."

She rolled her eyes. "Right. I can see how that would be a problem. Can you go fishing out there?"

He laughed. "Why am I not surprised you like to fish?"

"Hey, I'm a country girl. Some girls shop for clothes and

Skydiving to Love

jewelry, others shop for lures and reels."

"You want to go?"

She caught herself from bouncing in the seat like a toddler, and instead twisted partway around to see him. "Can we?"

"Sure. You want to fly back?"

It seemed rude to cut the flight short, and she was enjoying it. "Well, only if you do."

"Fine by me. Take the stick."

"Wait—*what*?"

"You'd better grab it before we crash."

She grabbed hold of the rubber grip with both hands, and the engine's vibrations shuddered up her arms. "What do I do?"

"Bring the nose up—pull the stick toward you."

She pulled and the plane responded with no more fuss than her old tractor, but with far more satisfaction. This was fun. "What now?"

Skydiving to Love

"Level it out," he said. "Push to make the nose go down, pull to get it up. Left, right—everything in between. I'll handle the rest."

She released a giddy laugh. "Am I really flying this thing?"

"Yep. How does it feel?"

"Invigorating!"

She turned the plane and went back, following the same landmarks he'd shown her and concentrating on keeping the wings level—not that it took much effort. Flying seemed easier than driving. No traffic to contend with. No stoplights or road construction. She just had to keep it level.

Before long, the small airport came into view. Fun time was about over, but a quick glance at the fuel gauge verified the fact that it was time to land.

"You ready to take over?" she asked.

"Nah. You're doing good. Wake me up back at the hangar."

Skydiving to Love

She shot a glance over her shoulder. "You're kidding! I can't land this thing!"

"You're right. I'm kidding."

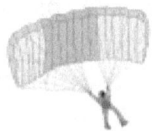

That evening, Mitch toasted her with his tea glass. "Not only can you catch them, you know what to do with them. Best fish dinner I've had in a long time."

"You did the beans." She shifted in her Adirondack chair in front of the fire pit and set her plastic plate on a wood-slat side table. He planned to spend the night and freshen up the place before his father returned for the weekend. She'd followed him from the city to the condo in her rental so she could leave whenever she got ready, but between the sounds of the lapping water and the singing crickets, she might never be ready.

Skydiving to Love

"Correction," he said. "I opened the can and nuked the beans. You did the hard stuff. Great fried fish. I even liked the coleslaw. My mom would've wanted your dressing recipe."

Inside the condo, she'd seen pictures of the O'Hara family. Mitch and another young man with their parents. Mitch, striking in his uniform. The O'Hara men had towered over Mary Beth, but the love and respect they'd held for her seemed evident in each photo. The differences between his family and her own were legion, especially after G-pop and Daddy died.

"I would've liked to meet her."

"You remind me of her." He grabbed a stick and placed it in the fire. The breeze blowing off the lake added a chill to the night air and sent tiny sparks winking away into the darkness. "She would've liked your spunk."

"Ha. Right. Wasn't that long ago you were calling me hysterical. And you weren't wrong."

Skydiving to Love

"Yeah, but you're a trooper. Think of everything we've done the past couple of days. The only thing missing was the jet noise."

"And the requirement to jump from the plane."

"Well, yes, there's that. Still, Mom would've liked you. Both my parents would."

He grew quiet, his gaze fixed on the fire, his tea glass held in both hands between his knees. Whatever was going on in his mind seemed to have taken him miles away, and she suddenly felt like an intruder.

She shifted her focus to the flames. She couldn't have asked for a more perfect day. Who knew she'd like flying so much? Okay, yes—Mitch knew somehow, just like he'd known how to keep her calm, how to protect her from the others' prying eyes after her episode on the Twin Otter. Just as he'd known to tease and compete with her on the water. His fish had been bigger, until she'd hauled in a whopper. He'd caught the most, until she landed two in a row and tied the score.

He'd gone from stranger to trusted friend in a matter of three days. An attractive, trusted friend whose touch she missed right now, but she hadn't reached the comfort level required to stretch over and take his hand. Though she did feel comfortable digging a little.

"What happened to your mother? How did she die?"

He studied his hands so long, she was afraid he wouldn't answer. Perhaps she shouldn't have asked. "Sorry. I didn't mean to pry."

He glanced at her. "No, it's all right. It was a long time ago. This place just ... reminds me of her, I guess. Makes me miss her." He leaned back and set his tea glass on the side table. "The official verdict was complications due to pneumonia."

"But you don't agree with the official verdict."

Skydiving to Love

"Not entirely." He took a deep breath through his nose and stared off into the night sky. "I believe she died of a broken heart."

JoJo waited for him to continue. Studied him. The crease in his brow, the sad droop of his lips. She'd known him only a short time, but seeing his sorrow so plainly written in the lines of his face hurt her heart.

Finally, he cut his eyes her way. "I had an older brother, Randall. He moved to Dallas after he graduated. Rand and Connie—his wife—were driving to Amarillo for Mom's birthday. Some teenager veered into his lane with one hand on the wheel of her daddy's Volvo and the other tapping a text on her cell phone. He swerved in front of a truck, the truck clipped them and sent them spinning into oncoming traffic. Connie was eight months pregnant."

JoJo winced. "Oh, wow. I'm so sorry."

Skydiving to Love

"Yeah, me too. They'd planned to move back to Amarillo. Mom had been fixing up a nursery at home, thinking she'd be called on to babysit my nephew—the baby was going to be a boy. After they died, she did too, in a way. Just checked out mentally before she finally checked out physically. But, like I said, that was a few years ago." He gave her a lopsided smile. "All right, mystery woman, it's time."

She laughed. "Mystery woman, huh? Okay, what is it time for?"

"Time for you to let me in on some of the mystery. You have yet to tell me anything substantial about yourself. I know you're a vet, that you don't want to jump, and you like to fish. Tell me something new."

"What do you want to know?"

"Start with how you came to be a large animal vet. No fluffy poodles for you, right? Bovine and equine all the way."

Skydiving to Love

"And goats. Don't forget the goats."

"And donkeys?"

"Of course. They're my favorite." She chuckled. "They were G-pop's favorite too. My grandfather was the reason I went into the field. He was a large-animal vet, James Herriot-style. When the ranchers couldn't bring their sick animals to him, he went to them. I spent a lot of time tramping through pastures, lugging whatever equipment and instruments I was big enough to carry, so I could watch G-pop work his magic."

"Did he raise you?"

That would've been great. "No."

He looked at her expectantly, studying her as she'd studied him. But she'd said as much as she dared, and now there was nothing left but awkward silence.

She didn't owe him anything, anyway—not like that. Not letting him in to her past and her secrets. After this week, she'd never see him again. After tonight, in fact. She could cut her vacation short and go home. She'd seen all she wanted of San Antonio.

She grabbed their plastic plates and rose. "Let me help you clean up."

He gave her a quizzical look as he stood. "There's not much to clean up."

He took the plates from her and tossed them into the fire, then took her hands. "Did I say something wrong?"

She looked at her hands enveloped in his. She'd spent the evening missing his touch, but now ... "No, it's just getting late. We've had a long day. I'm afraid it's catching up with me."

Skepticism clouded his eyes, but he kissed her softly on the cheek and draped his arm around her shoulders. "At least I can walk you to your car."

She fished her keys from her pocket as they walked, then

stopped at the car door. "I've had a great time, Mitch. You've made my vacation special."

"It's not over yet, is it? You're here till Friday, right?"

"I've taken enough of your time, haven't I? I was thinking I'd head home tomorrow."

"You're going to leave without giving skydiving another chance?"

She shrugged. "I'd have to conjure up another two hundred dollars. Not in my budget."

"Why don't you let me handle that?"

"I couldn't ask you to—"

"It's nothing." He waved away her protests. "Chad owes me. Why don't I set it up tomorrow and give you a call?"

She shuddered. "Tomorrow?"

"No? Okay, when, then?"

"Can I think about it?"

Skydiving to Love

He kissed her forehead. "I'll see you tomorrow."

JoJo paced the limited space of her hotel room, rolling her eyes at the gushing from the phone. She'd expected this kind of romanticism out of Annie, but Arabel? She'd always seemed more level-headed.

"He has a great car, his own plane, a condo on the lake, and enough clout in the city to treat you to a catered, roof-top dinner in the moonlight." Arabel sighed. "What a man."

"Yes, but I didn't come here to score a man." Especially not one who wanted to know everything about her.

"But you *did* score a man—and it doesn't hurt that he's rich. You'd never have to worry about money again. That college loan? *Poof!* It's gone!"

Skydiving to Love

"You make me sound like a gold digger." Even if she were to see him again after this week—which was doubtful—there was no *poof* in her future. She wouldn't let him pay her debts.

"Anyone who knows you knows better than that. But it doesn't hurt," she said again. "So are you seeing him tomorrow?"

JoJo flopped across the bed and fiddled open the mint that had been left on the pillow. "I don't know. He's already calling me mystery woman. Wants to know more about me."

"That's great!"

"With my past?"

"Oh, honey." Compassion oozed from her voice. "There's nothing in your past to be ashamed of."

"There's nothing in my past I want to share with a stranger, either." Besides, once he got to know her that well, he would lose interest right fast. She was too poor, from too rough of a background to hold a rich man's interest for long. Her home was

Skydiving to Love

far more humble than the condo she'd seen. And it suited her.

Arabel huffed. "Maybe you're chasing the wrong bucket-list item. Instead of jumping from a plane—something you never wanted to do anyway—you should be jumping into a relationship with a man you can confide in. He sounds like a great guy, maybe even the one God has planned for you."

"Oh, that's going a bit far, isn't it? I've known him less than a week!"

"Don't dismiss the idea entirely. Stranger things have happened—miraculous things." She took a sip of something, then continued. "Look, everything you've told me about him makes me believe you can trust him with your heart. Don't shut him out."

She was right to a certain extent. Mitch had a sense about him, a way of letting her know she could trust him. But how long would that hold true?

She popped the mint in her mouth and sat up, looking out the

Skydiving to Love

window at the skyline. Her bedroom window at home overlooked the pasture and the animals grazing there. "It doesn't matter anyway. He lives and works in the city. I live and work in the country eight hours away. It's not like I'll see him again after this."

"You never know. Have faith."

"Arabel—"

"Just promise me you'll give him a chance. It's only Wednesday. You'll never know what could happen if you turn tail and run now."

She shook her head. "Fine. Can we talk about you now?"

Chapter Nine

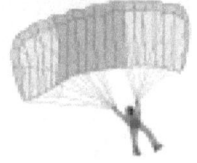

The sugar had probably dissolved long ago, but JoJo kept idly stirring her coffee and staring at the water rippling in the hotel swimming pool. She missed her stock pond at home, the quiet lapping of waves against the boat yesterday, the rolling current of the river. But this was available without her having to put on her makeup this morning or dress up in anything more formal than her shorts and tee. And it worked. Even chlorinated water in a concrete pond could offer peace to a frazzled mind.

Skydiving to Love

The opening bars to the chorus of "Stronger" erupted from her cell phone, the tune she'd designated for Kat. She grabbed the phone and answered.

"So," Kat said, "Arabel tells me you're getting cold feet about your honey-bunny."

"He's not my honey-bunny."

"But he wants to be."

JoJo huffed her bangs from her eyes. "I can't believe Arabel called the reinforcements."

"You'd better believe it." From the noises coming through the ear piece, it sounded like Kat had poured herself some coffee. "But you are changing the subject. What about this Mitch guy?"

"What about him?"

"He sounds great. You like him, don't you?"

"About as much as you like that hunk you're seeing right now."

Skydiving to Love

When Kat grew silent, JoJo laughed. "The shoe's on the other foot now, isn't it? You're as hesitant about your guy as I am about Mitch."

"Yes, but that's different."

"Not much different. We're both wounded warriors with our own set of baggage."

"And you don't think Mitch can handle yours?"

Could the king of surprises and *you'll see* handle a control-freak with more debt than time? Could a man with his happy family background handle her morbid history? Could anyone?

"That's not even an issue," she said. "Didn't Arabel tell you how far away I live from San Antonio? You do remember Texas, don't you? It's huge. Hours of driving and you never leave the state."

"She told me, and I do remember. But she also told me about the plane. He owns one, right?"

Skydiving to Love

"Doesn't mean he'd use it to fly to a podunk place like Hereford."

"You never know." A door opened and closed on Kat's end, keys jingled, and the background sounds changed. "I've got to get to the gym, but I wish you'd consider giving Mitch a chance. Even if nothing comes out of it, you could at least enjoy more time with him during the next couple of days."

"Have fun at the gym."

Kat laughed. "Fine. Be that way. Catch you later."

JoJo ended the call and tapped her phone against her palm. *Jump in*, Arabel had said. *You never know*, Kat had said. They made it sound so easy. But there was too much to overcome. Just too much ... Besides, she hadn't known Mitch long enough to see his own warts. What if the too-good-to-be-true adage fit? What if the skeletons in his closet were worse than the ones in hers?

She doubted it.

Skydiving to Love

The girls did have a point though. She'd be here a few more days. Might as well make the most of them.

She checked the time. Only seven. The hotel would be hopping soon with more visitors checking out or going down to take advantage of the breakfast or gym, and she had no inclination to do either. But flipping through morning news shows sounded less appealing. Mitch hadn't indicated when he'd call, but surely not this early. She grabbed a fresh cup of coffee from the bar inside and headed out the front for a walk.

The hotel's doors swished open, and she strolled through just as Mitch pulled his Audi into the circle drive. He'd ridden with the top down, and the wind through his hair had given him a casual, boyish look. Her heart pounded like a schoolgirl's.

Arabel and Kat were right. She'd been nuts to think she'd go home and miss out on another day with him.

He put the car in park. "Just who I came to see."

Skydiving to Love

She propped her fist on her hip and shot him a mock scowl. "I thought you were going to let me think about it. Maybe call first."

"Didn't want to give you a chance to back out."

"You didn't arrange something this early, did you?"

"By the time we get there, it won't be early." He killed the engine and stretched his arm across the back of the passenger seat. "Go get ready. I'll wait."

"You're just full of surprises, aren't you?" She shook her head. "Okay. I'll be down in a sec."

She retraced her steps back inside the hotel, dumped her coffee—there were no bathrooms on the Twin Otter—and headed for the elevator. The door slid open, she stepped in, poked her floor number, and slumped against the wall.

This was it. Could she do it?

The door opened on her floor. She pulled her keycard from

her pocket as she walked down the hall.

Mitch had proven she had nothing to be afraid of. She didn't have vertigo—she could've told him that—wasn't afraid of heights, didn't get dizzy when looking down. Flying in his sweet little put-put plane yesterday had actually been relaxing. The Twin Otter had two propellers, so it was a little louder, but that was a good thing. It had more power. It wouldn't crash. And she hadn't been sucked out when the door opened. Another good thing. Those fears were irrational.

Right?

Inside her room, she changed from her summer casuals to something more suitable for jumping from a plane. Her skinny jeans and a snug shirt to fit under the jumpsuit, and some socks to wear with her jogging shoes. She sat on the ottoman to lace up her shoes.

Mitch had said that once the canopy opened, it was like flying in the Piper Cub, but much quieter. Wind noise without engine noise. And no oil or plane fuel smells. She'd liked the Piper Cub. She needed to remember that.

A couple of minutes in front of the mirror to yank her hair into a ponytail and settle a cap on top, and she was ready to go.

But she stopped on her way out, with her hand on the doorknob.

She wanted to do this. She *needed* to do this. She'd told everyone she would, so she was obligated to do this. But could she do it?

She raised her chin. Yes. She could. If Kat could climb a mountain, if Annie could crash a famous wedding, she could jump from a plane.

Her shoulders slumped. That little pep talk sounded familiar, and it hadn't worked the first time. If only she could talk to Annie this morning to be fortified by her strength. What would she tell her to do? *Take a breath, say a prayer, step out on faith.*

She sucked air in through her nose and shoved it out through her lips. *Father, for some reason I don't understand, this is important to me. Please help me do it.*

She squared her shoulders and jerked open the door.

Then dashed back to grab her keycard.

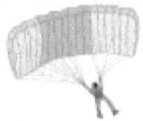

itch leaned into her. "You okay?"

She nodded with a confidence she didn't quite feel. They shared the cabin with Chad, who gave her an encouraging smile every time he caught her eye. He was probably bracing himself for another round with her hysteria.

But she'd done pretty well with the takeoff, and the engine noise didn't bother her. No reason it should, really. Prop engines sounded different from jet engines. No high-pitched whining. So, at least as far as going up in a propeller plane, Mitch had succeeded in ridding her of her fear of flying. Would her newfound confidence extend to the jet that would fly her home? That remained to be seen.

Mitch took her hand, rubbing his thumb over the back of it, and reminded her of how the buddy jump would go. Again. He'd touched on it during the drive out to the airport, had reminded her as they suited up and headed for the plane, and now, again. As if he was just as nervous as she. And if he kept it up, her nervous tension would amp up another level.

"I know." She placed her other hand on top of his. "I'm okay."

He gave her a pride-filled look and kissed her fingers. The gesture made her heart skip a beat. She couldn't let him down.

But when the yellow light flickered on over the cockpit, her nerves jerked tight. Chad rose and pulled the door open, and her

Skydiving to Love

pulse raced.

Mitch squeezed her hand. "Still good?"

She bobbed her head and lied. "Yeah."

They stood. Chad came and checked her straps, then stood back so Mitch could connect with her.

She twisted away. "I can't."

She strode with long steps back toward the tail of the plane—then pounded the wall and plopped onto the bench.

He sat beside her. "You don't have to do this."

"Yes I do."

"I don't understand. This isn't a matter of life or death. It's for pleasure. And if you don't find it pleasurable, then why are you taking it so hard?"

"Because I said I would. I keep my word. I *always* keep my word."

"That's admirable, but this isn't important, honey. It's

supposed to be fun."

"Doesn't matter." She shifted toward him. "Look, you wanted to know more about me, here it is. Before G-pop died, I promised I'd take over his practice someday, and I did. Before Daddy died, I promised I'd take care of Mom, and I did—or I tried. But the money G-pop left for me was invested until I turned twenty-five, and Dad's health bills ate up what we had. Mom didn't work, didn't know what to do with herself. She just stayed drunk until she died of cirrhosis three years ago."

His eyes filled with sympathy, but she couldn't stand his pity. She stood and paced in the tiny space to keep from looking at him. "When I was fourteen, I faked an ID and worked at a Kroger after school, checking steaks and seafood and fancy vegetables all day, then I'd take home Ramen Noodles and frozen peas to feed myself and my mom each night. I saved all I could, then worked my way through college, through grad school. I kept my word to

Daddy and G-pop. I always keep my word."

"But this isn't like that, JoJo. It isn't life or death. It's not important."

She whirled toward him. "It is to me!" She took a breath to settle the frantic anger rising in her chest, then lowered her voice. "I don't understand why, but it is important to me."

"All right, then." He stood and took her by the shoulders. "You've always done things all by yourself. But you don't have to now. You have me. You've trusted me all week. Trust me a little longer." He slid his hands down her arms. "Lean on me. Rely on me. Relinquish your control just long enough to trust me. We can keep your word together."

She studied him, the intensity reflected in his eyes, the determination showing in the set of his jaw, and nodded. "Okay. Let's do this before I lose my resolve."

"Yes!" He hugged her, gave her a resounding smack on the

lips, then twirled a finger in the air and shouted to Chad, "Circle the drop zone. We're jumping!"

Chad relayed the message to the pilot, then checked her straps again. As Mitch hooked them together, the yellow light switched to green, and Chad pulled the door open. Wind filled the fuselage, and she sucked down as much of it as she could. Mitch felt firm and solid against her back. But trusting him was a challenge as he walked her closer to the opening.

She pulled her goggles over her eyes. *This is it, Lord. I'm trusting this man you sent my way. Please keep us safe.*

He rubbed her shoulders. "You'll love this. Really, you will. I'm excited for you."

She nodded and leaned back to yell in his ear. "Just don't drop me."

Chad held up a finger, then his thumb, then, "Go!"

She did everything as she'd been taught—crossed her arms

over her chest, tucked her legs when he stepped out. And fell.

The sensation of free-falling thrilled her like nothing she'd ever experienced. When Mitch signaled her, she straightened—arms and legs out—and rushed through the air like some masked superhero charging toward Earth. A hundred twenty miles per hour, he'd said. One hundred twenty from ten thousand feet in the air.

Laughter bubbled up from the pit of her stomach and erupted through her lips. She couldn't stop it if she'd wanted, and she didn't want to. She had no control over the gravity pulling them toward earth, no control of the wind speed—no control at all. Just faith and trust and a release she'd never allowed herself to experience. And she felt giddy with the joy of it.

Just over a minute of free-falling, then Mitch pulled the ripcord. The drag of the canopy being deployed gave her the sensation of going upward, of being jerked back into the atmosphere. They'd slowed from their rapid speed to thirty miles per hour. The wind noise softened at this speed, no longer rushing past her ears.

The patchwork landscape seemed even more breathtaking with no obstruction to her view. The river that ultimately wound its way through San Antonio, the highway, with its ant-like cars zipping down it—and the drop zone, signaling the end of the jump.

"Ready to land?" Mitch asked in her ear.

No, she wanted to stay up forever. But, gravity being what gravity was, she crossed her arms and tucked her legs.

He toggled the canopy, and they slowed more. Soon he was running to a stop on the tarmac, and her experience ended.

Still effervescent with laughter, she jerked off her goggles and squealed.

He disconnected them, and she threw her arms around him.

Skydiving to Love

"What a rush! I've never felt anything so liberating."

"I knew you'd love it." He rested his hands at the small of her back.

The excitement shining from his eyes shifted to—what? Curiosity? Longing? Whatever it was, in that instant, she felt the same. His lips were nearer to hers than they'd ever been, and sampling them would be just a matter of tilting her head ...

His kiss—soft, tentative, probing—sent her head reeling back into the clouds. The heat off the tarmac rose and amped the flame he himself caused by pulling her closer, holding her tighter. She'd stumble if he let go. Her legs wouldn't hold her. Passion flared, urgency demanded—

And that scared her.

She rested her hand on his cheek—still smooth from the morning's shave—and pulled away. Just a little. Not so far she couldn't taste him again with the least effort. She traced his jaw and dared to raise her eyes to see the hunger smoldering in his.

Then he shifted his gaze over her shoulder and stepped back. He shouted and waved at Chad, who jogged toward them.

Mitch held up her arm in victory. "She did it!"

"That was awesome! I'm excited for you." Chad leaned toward her and kissed her cheek. "Well, what do you think? Ready to go up again?"

She glanced between him and Mitch. "Could we?"

Mitch laughed. "That's up to Chad and the pilot."

Chad studied her for a moment. "You think you liked it well enough to go solo?"

Mitch raised his brow at the question and turned to her. "I'll be with you all the way. We just won't be connected—not like that, anyway."

"What do you mean?"

"Well," he gestured between himself, her, and Chad, "the

three of us can jump together and hold wrists on the way down."

"Like in the pictures I saw."

"Yeah, like that. You game?"

The buddy jump had been amazing, breathtaking. Second only to kissing Mitch O'Hara. Could she jump without him?

If she didn't do it now, she'd never get another chance, a thought that bothered her more than she'd expected. But now, the bucket-list dare she hadn't even wanted became the thing she wanted to do most.

"I'm in!"

Chapter Ten

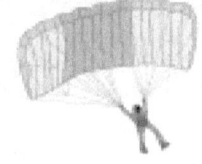

JoJo almost hated to jump into the shower. It would be too much like washing the day away. The smell of the fuel and the oil and the air. And Mitch. The invigorating sensation of free-falling, the feel of Chad and Mitch clasping her wrists. The sound of the wind, the sound of their laughter. The tug of her canopy as she toggled to her landing. Not a very good one, not at all graceful. Still, she hadn't broken anything.

But worse, the shower would wash away the feel of Mitch's

arms around her. The taste of his lips as he explored her own.

She hadn't experienced anything so heady since Stewart Youngblood kissed her in the stables back when she was an undergrad. She'd been a college junior before she experienced the magic of a kiss. They'd dated off and on for years. Studied together as both pursued a degree in veterinary medicine. But with her studies, her full time job, and her frequent trips home to tend to her mother, she hadn't been able to make it work.

Now, she was in the same boat. With her practice and the distance between Hereford and San Antonio, she and Mitch would never get to see each other.

She tested the water, then climbed in under the spray. She'd been foolish to let things escalate between them anyway. She needed to rein in her heart. After tomorrow, she'd never see him again. Probably after tonight.

But she still had tonight.

Skydiving to Love

She dried and styled her hair, applied her makeup with more care than usual, then sifted through the clothes she'd brought with her. If she'd shopped this afternoon instead of jumping from a plane again, she'd have something different and more appropriate to wear. The only classy-looking outfit she had was the one she'd bought the other day. She sighed and slipped into it.

At least this time, she could wear the heels.

She rode the elevator down to wait for him in the lobby, but he was already there, lounging in one of the chairs with a bouquet of long-stem roses resting in his lap. More red than yellow. The romance between them would be short lived. She'd have to let him down easy.

He saw her and rose from his chair, almost dropping the flowers. He gathered them together in a haphazard bundle, then crossed to meet her. "You look great."

"You said that the first time I wore this outfit."

Skydiving to Love

"Meant it then, mean it now." He lightly brushed his lips against hers. "Hope you still like roses."

She accepted them and brought them to her nose. Sweet, intoxicating. Just like the man who'd given them to her. "Still do."

He nodded toward the sliding glass doors. "Ready?"

"Just a moment." She stopped at the desk and asked the concierge to put the roses in water and send them to her room. With his assurance, she left them with him and rejoined Mitch. "Ready."

He'd put the top up on the beautiful blue Audi, which was fine to keep her hair from blowing, but she'd miss riding in the convertible and feeling the wind on her face. They drove only a few blocks to a steakhouse and went inside a restaurant that smelled like grilled beef, wine, and class. She shuddered to think how much money he'd spent on her today alone. Finding a rich man had never been one of her goals—finding a *man* had been

Skydiving to Love

put on the back burner until her college loan was paid off—but being treated like a princess did have its perks.

Even if it was just for one more night.

He gave his name to the hostess, who seated them at a candle-lit table out of the way of traffic and left them with their menus. He held her chair for her, then settled beside her.

"I know you work on cattle, but are you opposed to eating beef?—aside from hamburgers, that is."

She laughed. "No, that's one of the ways I keep my ranchers in business."

"Good." He opened his menu. "If you'd like a suggestion what to have, try the Brazilian Picanha. It's out of this world. A top sirloin cap coated with rock salt and flame-grilled to perfection. You don't want to miss it."

"You've been right about everything else during my entire vacation, so I'm happy to take your advice."

Skydiving to Love

A waiter came and offered the wine list. Mitch raised a questioning brow at her.

Well, why not? She wasn't much of a wine drinker, but this was the last day of her vacation. One glass wouldn't hurt. "The house white will be fine."

He ordered a Pinot Grigio for her and a Merlot for himself, then placed the dinner order.

After the waiter left, Mitch took her hand and played with her fingers. "I've been thinking about what you said earlier."

"What's that?"

"About you working your way through college and about keeping your word. About your mom."

She winced. Had she really spilled her entire past to him? She shook her head. "I'm sorry. I didn't mean to dump on you."

"No, don't apologize. I admire you." He shifted from playing with her fingers to tracing the veins on the back of her hand and focused on the movement. "Rand and I had it easy. We were both spoiled rotten. Mom and Dad were ... well, let's just say they had several healthy investments and a couple of nice, hefty accounts. I had the attitude of an affluenza kid before the Air Force knocked it out of me."

She glanced around their surroundings, then raised a brow at him. "So now, you're just a regular Joe?"

He released a sardonic laugh. "Not entirely. But at least I don't expect everything to be handed to me anymore. What I have now, I've worked for." He paused for a moment. "But meeting you, realizing how hard you've worked to get what you want—that's humbled me. I can't imagine ... "

Her cheeks grew hot, and she turned away. What was she supposed to say to this? What was he doing? Offering her—what? Sympathy? Pity?

"I'm botching this all up, aren't I?" He paused while the waiter set wine glasses before them and filled each one. After he left, Mitch shifted toward her. "All I mean is that I admire you. I've never met anyone like you."

Had he realized that before he'd discovered she was poor, or after? She bit back a sarcastic remark and reached for her wine. "Well, that's me. One of a kind."

His lips tightened into a grim line for an instant as he reached for his own goblet, then he smiled. "So, what's next on your bucket list? Anything that competes with skydiving?"

Small talk. After everything they'd gone through together, they would now revert to small talk.

She sighed inwardly. "I really don't know. I've been living my bucket list." She laughed. "I just hope the girls don't dare each other again. It's turning out to be more than I can take."

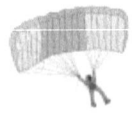

Skydiving to Love

He drove her back to the hotel after dinner, but pulled into a parking place instead of the circle drive. He killed the engine, then kept both hands on the wheel.

"Look," he said, staring out the windshield. "I know everything I said came out wrong earlier. All I meant was that I admire you. You probably think I'm a Class A jerk now."

"Oh, no." She twisted in her seat to face him. "You've made my vacation special. I appreciate everything you've done for me. And to top it off with that fabulous meal—I won't have to eat for a week."

"I figured you'd like it." He stretched his arm across the back of her seat and massaged her neck gently. "I guess you're leaving tomorrow?"

"Yes. Have to get back to my cinders and ashes before my rental carriage turns into a pumpkin," she said, then winced at the poor-girl-rich-prince reference.

Skydiving to Love

He chuckled. "I guess I deserved that."

"No, you didn't. And I didn't mean it that way. I was just trying to be funny." Maybe in the darkness of evening, he couldn't see her blush. "I didn't realize how it would sound until it popped out of my mouth."

"I guess we're even then." He kissed her fingers.

"I guess we are," she murmured. With his head bent over her hand, all she wanted to do was run her fingers through his hair. Caress that strong jaw again. Bring his lips to hers. "I guess I need to go in and start packing. I have an early flight."

"I can drive you."

"Thank you, but no. I need to return the rental."

"Next time I'm in Amarillo—"

"Mitch." She shook her head. "I loved my time with you, and I'd love to see you again, but I don't see how it would work. I'm up before dawn, in bed at dark. Sometimes I'm called out during the night. Once I get back to my real world, I won't have time for anything else. And with the miles between us ... Well, you know about long-distance relationships."

Again his lips formed that tight line. He glanced out the windshield for a moment. Cars passed, headlights reflected off street signs. Ahead, the traffic signal turned green and a pickup swung into the parking lot, sweeping them in the truck's twin beams.

Mitch focused on her again, then pulled her into his arms and kissed her. A soft, tender kiss that made her want to take back everything she'd said. Then he pulled away, releasing her and leaving her with a dazed heart and dizzy head.

"I'd better escort you in." He softly traced her cheek. "I've really enjoyed meeting you."

Chapter Eleven

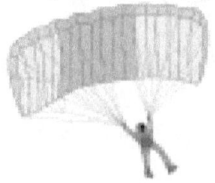

JoJo peeled off the shoulder-length vinyl gloves and gave the cow a pat on the rump. The problem pregnancy had resulted in healthy twin Charolais calves, and the mom should recover nicely.

Kyle Hanson shoved his hands in his back pockets and watched the calves nurse for a few moments, then turned to her. "You done for the day?"

Skydiving to Love

"So far as I know." She pulled her phone from her pocket. Six-thirty, and no messages. Hot diggity. "I'm getting off early."

"Gettin' off early on a Friday night. Not too bad. Want to go to the dance?"

He'd been asking her out for ages. With his boyish smile, blond hair, and smattering of freckles, not many girls would turn him down, but she didn't hesitate to shake her head.

"I've been up since four-thirty. All I've got in mind is a long bath and a good book. With any luck, I'll be asleep by eight."

He flashed her his famous smile. "Someday you're going to say yes."

She laughed and dug in her jeans pocket for her keys. "Sure. As soon as I can afford to hire a couple of helpers and an accountant and work normal hours."

He walked her to her pickup. "You know what they say about all work."

Skydiving to Love

"Yes." She climbed in and put the key in the ignition. "All work and no sleep will make JoJo unemployed."

She cranked up and tossed a wave out the window as she followed the truck ruts back to the gate. At the blacktop, she turned left and headed home. Fortunately, Kyle's family ranch wasn't too far from her own little farmhouse.

She stopped at the mailbox before turning into her drive. Tyke and Balsa dashed off the front porch and barked their greetings, bouncing at her truck door. She squeezed out of the pickup and succumbed to the sloppy kisses of her two mutts—one a poodle/beagle/jack-russell-looking thing with floppy ears and a curly beagle-colored coat, and the other some kind of mountain breed mixed with a touch of spaniel and colored like a German shepherd. Loyal, loveable companions who guarded her and her home. She roughhoused with them for a few minutes, then walked around to the back porch and grabbed some carrots from a bin.

Bray and Susie were waiting for her at the pasture gate. The moment Bray saw her, he hee-hawed and bobbed his head. Susie nudged his neck as if telling him to settle down, and he nipped at her. The two donkeys were inseparable, but all bets were off when it came to carrots.

"You two are crazy, you know that?" She handed them each a treat, then scratched their ears and necks.

A small airplane flew overhead, its wings glinting in the evening sun. She shaded her eyes and watched until it flew out of sight, a tiny speck on the peaches-and-cream horizon. She'd been home for three weeks, but still the sight of a plane made her wistful even as it pumped her adrenaline.

Her flight home had been far different from the one to San Antonio. Excitement rather than fear had tightened her nerves, but melancholy had laden her heart. She'd probably never get to

Skydiving to Love

fly again. Never see Mitch again.

That pained her far more than a week-long relationship should have. She missed him. The more she thought about him—and she thought of him often—the more she realized what a treasure he was. Who else would have taken so much time to try to ease her mind about flying? To explore her fears with her? To take her fishing?

Skydiving had been great, invigorating. And she'd kept her promise about doing it. Keeping her word still felt important to her, but the girls had been right. She should've let herself dive into a relationship with Mitch. Should've waited to see what would happen. Anything was better than this emptiness she felt without him.

But it was too late now. She'd shut down any chance for love before it could start. What choice did she have? Her lifestyle, the distance between them, didn't allow for any kind of relationship to develop. Best to sever ties before they became too tight. She'd done the right thing.

She gave Bray's muzzle a final rub, then turned toward the animal hospital, such as it was. So much equipment was needed before it could be a true clinic, but she had the basics. At least enough to house a couple of colicky horses. She stepped into the coolness of the horse barn—her hospital—and cooed at Adrian, a seven-year-old quarter horse with milk-chocolate eyes that seemed a bit brighter today. Just as she reached for the stall gate, the dogs darted away in a barking frenzy. She followed them out. Someone must've pulled into the drive. Heaven help her if her mutts clambered all over a client like they did her.

But instead of rushing to the driveway, the dogs charged toward a figure in the pasture.

She caught her breath and gaped at him.

Mitch released his harness from the chute and strolled over to

Skydiving to Love

her. "You're a hard lady to find."

It took her a moment to kick her brain into gear. Then finally, "How did you find me?"

She'd never given him so much as her phone number, much less directions to her home.

"It took some sleuthing. Chad gave me a peek at your sign-up info, then I had to find your address on the internet maps and then check the flight charts." He dumped the chute and stepped closer to her. "Sorry it took me so long to get here. I was in Brazil for a couple of weeks, then Chad couldn't get off to fly me out here. I could've taken the Cub, but then I wouldn't have had this dramatic moment of falling from the sky to see you."

She couldn't wrap her mind around what was happening. Mitch stood in her pasture, still in his jumpsuit, grinning like a kid with a secret—and she'd just been thinking of him.

He tilted his head. "Say something."

153

Skydiving to Love

"I—" she paused, trying to formulate a coherent sentence. "I didn't think I'd see you again."

"Yeah, about that. You're overruled. I can't handle the idea of never seeing you again." He closed the distance between them and slipped his arms around her waist. "Look, I travel a lot. My job takes me all over the world, but my home base can be anywhere God puts me. Even here in Hereford, if you want me."

Her heart leapt. "Yes, I do. I want you. I want to be able to see you on a regular basis." She caressed the stubbled cheek of the man God had brought into her life. "There's a farmhouse for rent up the road. We don't get delivery out here, but come see me anytime. I make a killer pizza."

"Sounds like a deal. I know I'll love my neighbor." He studied her eyes, her lips, making her breath catch and her heart pound. "You don't know how much I've missed you."

He pulled her closer, held her tighter—then something jabbed her ribs.

She stepped back. "What is that?"

"Oh, I forgot." He pulled a side zipper and extracted a rectangular box from his jump suit. "Thought you might like this."

The plain brown box was about a foot long and six inches high. "What is it?"

"Open it."

She slid a nail through the tape and opened the top. Inside, nestled in Styrofoam, a Mexican ceramic colt glanced up at her—blue head, olive green ears, rust-colored mane, red legs, and vivid blue flowers on his sides.

"I thought he'd like a home in Hereford."

"And what about you?" She searched his eyes. "Will you be happy here?"

He returned to his place in her arms. "That depends on you.

Ready to jump?"

She ran her fingers through the hair at the nape of his neck and murmured, "Hitch me to your harness. I'm ready."

The End

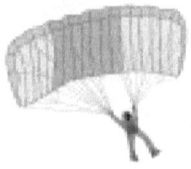

Love Comes on a Dare

Skydiving to Love was originally part of an interlocking four-novella collection, known as The Bucket List Dare. Each of the friends mentioned have their own stories to tell ...

The four best friends—each facing their thirtieth birthday—challenge each other to revisit the bucket list they made in college and tackle one daring item before they turn thirty. Living in different parts of the country, they choose their adventure and work toward making it happen ... with wonderful, unexpected results.

Her Impossible Dream, by Angela Breidenbach: Arabel Milligan, recently unemployed and with a new genealogical

Skydiving to Love

certification to her name, takes off for Scotland to discover the answer to a mysterious missing branch in her ancestral tree.

***Save the Groom*, by Jessica Ferguson**: Annie Flowers, a wedding photographer whose reputation is her pride and her job is her life, crashes the most extravagant wedding in the country.

***What Lies Ahead*, by Pamela S. Meyers**: Kat Brownlee, an army veteran and amputee, has always dreamed of climbing the most challenging mountain she could find. Now that her life and body have been drastically altered—does she dare?

***Skydiving to Love*, by Linda W. Yezak**: JoJo Merritt is a country veterinarian who has never jumped out of anything higher than a hayloft much less an airplane. How did that get on her bucket list?

These young professionals went out in search of adventure, but they also found love.

Each novella will release in 2018 on Amazon.

About the Author

Linda W. Yezak lives with her amazing husband and pudgy cat PB in a forest in east Texas, a God-kissed place of tall tales and shameless exaggeration. When she's not writing, she's reading, cooking, or cross-stitching baby blankets for each of her new grandkids. Her favorite activities are fishing, attending sporting events, and hanging out with friends and family.

More than anything, Linda loves to write. Her first novel, *Give the Lady a Ride*, won the 2011 Grace Award for Romance and was a finalist for American Christian Fiction Writer's Carol Award. Its sequel, *The Final Ride* won the Texas Association of Authors' Best in Fiction Award for Christian Fiction. Her first short story, "Slider," received an honorable mention in *Saturday Evening Post's* 2015 "Great American Fiction Contest."

Skydiving to Love

Special Thanks

To Katie Weiland and Cathilyn Dyck, whose eagle eyes catch a multitude of errors.

To Lynnette Bonner, who works magic and creates amazing book covers.

To Jessica Ferguson, who provided the idea of these dare-devil women and their bucket lists.

And to my Heavenly Father for bringing all these wonderful people into my life.

161

Books by Linda W. Yezak

The Circle Bar Ranch Series:

Give the Lady a Ride
The Final Ride
Coming soon: *Ride to the Altar*

Stand-Alone Fiction

The Cat Lady's Secret

The Simulacrum
(with Brad Seggie)

Nonfiction:

Writing in Obedience
(with Terry Burns)

The Circle-Bar Ranch Series

(Coming in 2018: *Ride to the Altar*)

Special note from the author

Authors live for reviews–and reviews keep authors alive and working. If you enjoyed this, or any of my novels, please let others know. Reviews on Amazon bring sweetness to my life!

If you'd like to get first notice of my newest releases, sign up for my "Coffee with Linda" newsletter: http://lindawyezak.com